The Wish Fairy

perfectly Popular

ALSO BY LISA ANN SCOTT

The Wish Fairy

ENCHANTED PONY ACADEMY

The Wish Fairy

perfectly Popular

Lisa Ann Scott

illustrated by
Heather Burns

SCHOLASTIC INC.

The publisher does not have any control over and does not assume any responsibility for author or third-party websites or their content.

ISBN 978-1-338-12102-5

10 9 8 7 6 5 4 3 2   18 19 20 21 22

Printed in the U.S.A.   40

First printing 2018

Book design by Yaffa Jaskoll

To my fun, lovely nieces,
Brooke and Izzy.
Hope all your wishes come true.

Chapter 1

Brooke sat near the pond in the middle of town with her best friend, Izzy, and their fairy friend, Calla. Just a few days earlier, she had saved Calla from her cat, Patches. Calla had to grant Brooke seven wishes in return! So far, Brooke had made three of them, and they had all come true. But they hadn't turned out like she'd expected.

Making good wishes was much harder than it seemed. Her first wish had been for one hundred cats. But Brooke soon figured out that all of the cats—except one—belonged to someone else! So she'd spent another wish to return them, and Izzy adopted the last cat, Pumpkin.

Next, Brooke wished for buried gold to appear in her meadow. But once people found out about it, everyone wanted it—even a dragon! All the treasure hunters had damaged her lovely meadow searching for more coins. The bank in town thought the loot was from a long-ago robbery and wanted to keep it. Donating everything to the library was the only way to end the madness—and it saved the library from closing. Still, that was not the perfect wish Brooke had imagined.

Now she had four more wishes to make. And she was determined not to mess things up again.

"I've decided I'm done wishing for *stuff*," Brooke told Izzy and Calla.

"This sounds interesting," Calla said.

"I'm confused." Izzy laughed. "What are you going to wish for, then?"

Brooke grinned up at the sun. "Something special. Something you can't buy. Something I'll be so proud of. I should really be using these wishes to make my life better, not just to *get* things, you know?"

"That sounds awesome." Izzy jumped up, scattering the tiny flowers she'd been picking. "What would make your life better?"

She held out a hand and pulled Brooke up from the ground.

"I'm tired of being invisible," Brooke said, brushing off her shorts. "I want everyone at school to know who I am."

"You know how to turn invisible?" Calla asked. "I can't even do that."

Brooke laughed. "No, I mean most people never even notice me. I want to change that."

"How can you make that happen?" Izzy asked.

"I want to be an amazing singer." Brooke flung her arms wide open and took a bow.

"That's a wonderful wish," Izzy said.

"But I have to get the wording right." Brooke rehearsed the wish in her head. For her last wish, she'd asked for buried gold to

appear in her meadow—but when the wish came true, the gold was still buried! It took a long time to find it.

So, perfect wording was a must when making wishes. She took a deep breath, then announced, "Calla, I wish I could sing the music solo for the school concert perfectly, and be the star of the last show of the year." *That was specific enough, right?*

Izzy gasped. "Tryouts are tomorrow!"

"I know!" Brooke said. "Perfect timing."

Calla twirled up into the air. "A most unusual wish, but it is indeed one that I can fulfill." With a flick of her wand, a flash of glitter appeared. "Your wish has been granted."

Brooke touched her throat. She didn't

feel any different. Her lips weren't tingling. Beautiful words didn't flow out of her mouth. "I'm not sure that worked."

"You won't know until you try. Sing the song!" Izzy demanded.

They'd all practiced the song in music class, but Brooke didn't know it by heart. She sang the first few words, "Send me a rainbow . . ." and the rest of the words came rushing out, all in perfect pitch, in the loveliest voice. She never dreamed she could sound so wonderful.

Izzy's eyes widened and her jaw dropped. "Brooke! That was amazing! You're going to be a star!" She grabbed Brooke's hands and they jumped up and down together.

Brooke giggled and sang the song again.

It still sounded incredible. She couldn't believe it! Finally, she'd made a perfect wish.

Calla brushed her hands together. "I'm rather good at this wish-granting business. While I was embarrassed at first to be discovered by a human, I'm grateful now that I've had a chance to put my skills to the test.

I dare say I'm the best wish granter in the history of Fairvana."

"I'm sure you are!" Izzy said.

"And I've finally gotten the hang of picking the right wish," Brooke said. "Nothing can go wrong with this one."

Brooke couldn't stop grinning as they walked home. Tomorrow was going to be an amazing day.

Chapter 2

Brooke spent the night tossing and turning, so excited about her new talent that she couldn't sleep. Wouldn't her music teacher, Mrs. Collins, be surprised?

In the morning, as Brooke packed her backpack, Calla crept out of the dollhouse where she'd been sleeping. "Which dress should I wear to school?" She held up two tiny, fancy gowns.

"You can't come to school! There are

hundreds of kids there. Aren't you afraid of being discovered?" Brooke asked.

Calla shook her head as she put on one of the doll dresses. "I'm not missing a trip to school! This research is essential for the *Humans in Their Natural Environment* book I'm writing."

Sighing, Brooke put on a sweatshirt. She held open one of the big pockets. "Get in. But I have a bad feeling you're going to get us both in trouble."

Calla somersaulted through the air, diving right into the pocket. "Can you get me some snacks?"

Brooke laughed, shaking her head. "For a tiny creature, you sure do eat a lot."

As she dashed through the kitchen on

her way to the bus, Brooke slipped a chocolate chip cookie in her pocket and a few in her backpack. Calla squealed and Brooke could hear her happily eating all the way to school.

Keeping Calla hidden was a good distraction as Brooke waited for music class, which was just after lunch. Calla squirmed around

in the pocket during math, and poked her head out in the middle of art class.

Brooke gently poked it back in, and was rewarded with a tiny kick to her thumb.

During a movie on the pyramids in world studies, their teacher, Mrs. Warner, turned off the lights. Calla climbed out of her pocket and sat on Brooke's desk to watch. Brooke propped her elbows on either side of the fairy so no one could see her. "I told you to stay in the pocket."

"That's fairy abuse!" Calla whispered.

The girl sitting next to her looked over, and Brooke faked a cough. What in the world would kids in class do if they saw Calla? Brooke wasn't sure having a distraction was worth all this trouble!

By the time her class filed into the music room, Brooke was so excited and nervous that her stomach was churning. She took a seat in the first row and Izzy sat next to her and squeezed her hand. "Good luck!" her friend whispered.

"Thanks!" Even though Brooke knew the words would come out perfectly, she wasn't used to being the center of attention. This was scary!

Lucy Jones sat at the end of the first row, gripping her folder. Everyone knew Lucy was the best singer in class.

Well, everyone is about to be very surprised.

"Good afternoon, class," Mrs. Collins said. "I know you've all been working hard on our headline song, 'Send Me a Rainbow.' Today, we're going to choose the person who gets to sing that as the solo during our concert this Thursday! Please come to the front of the room if you'd like to audition."

Brooke was so anxious, she felt hot. She jumped up from her seat and took off her sweatshirt. She heard a small squeak.

Izzy picked it up and put it on, gently patting the pocket where Calla sat, and would hopefully stay put.

Brooke stood next to Lucy. "Good luck," Lucy whispered to Brooke.

"You too." Brooke felt a little guilty

knowing Lucy didn't have a chance to win the solo. Not after Brooke's wish.

Lucy was first in line. She sang the song in a strong, beautiful voice. The girl and two boys standing next to Brooke slumped their shoulders as they listened to her.

Mrs. Collins clapped when Lucy finished. "Lovely, just lovely."

"Thanks," Lucy said. "I've been practicing every day."

"I can tell," Mrs. Collins said. "Hard work always pays off!"

Lucy grinned and nodded.

"Okay, next up is Brooke!"

Brooke hoped she'd be able to sing and smile at the same time. She was so happy and excited for everyone to hear her new gift!

Mrs. Collins started playing and Brooke began singing. "Send me a rainbow..." The words poured out of her mouth perfectly.

Mrs. Collins gasped and stopped playing the piano, her eyes wide and fingers poised over the keys.

Brooke looked over at Izzy and spotted Calla flying above the students to the top of the window at the back of the room.

"I can't believe it," Mrs. Collins said.

Brooke froze. How could she explain why a fairy was in the room?

"I've never . . ." Mrs. Collins said.

Brooke's mind raced. Should she pretend she'd seen a dragonfly? That's what she'd thought Calla was the first time she'd spotted her in the meadow. Or should she just keep singing? She turned to Izzy and they shared a desperate look.

"I'm sorry," Mrs. Collins said. "It's just that I've never heard such a lovely singing voice in a student your age."

Brooke sighed and then giggled. "Oh! Oh, okay. You're just . . . you didn't . . . I mean, thanks. Shall I finish?"

"Yes, of course!" Mrs. Collins continued playing. When Brooke was done, the teacher hurried over and set her hands on Brooke's shoulders. "That was amazing."

The kids who were still lined up to audition took their seats.

"Aren't you going to try out?" Mrs. Collins asked them.

"Nope," one of them said. "There's no way I'm better than Brooke." The two other kids nodded in agreement.

A soft whistling came from the back of the room. Brooke didn't have to look to know who was making the noise.

Mrs. Collins grinned. "Sounds like the birds were inspired by you, too, Brooke."

"Yep, those are birds. Definitely birds." Brooke forced a laugh while Izzy turned to glare at Calla.

"I think the birds have spoken. Brooke, you're going to sing the solo at the concert!"

Mrs. Collins beamed at Brooke. "I've never heard a voice like yours."

"Thanks!" Brooke smiled so wide it hurt. Until she saw Lucy's sad face. Then her smile faded, knowing how disappointed Lucy was.

But Lucy always had the spotlight song in all the concerts. Finally, Brooke had a chance to shine, and she was going to enjoy it!

Chapter 3

At the end of class, Calla was still sitting on top of the window frame, so Izzy went to fetch her.

Lucy appeared beside Brooke as the students headed for the door. "Where did you learn to sing like that? Did you hire a private teacher? I've wanted to, but we don't have the money. I'm saving up, though. I want to be a singer on Broadway someday." She looked off dreamily.

"No, I didn't work with a teacher," Brooke said. "I just . . . it just came out like that."

"My grandma came over from China for the summer. She'll be at the concert. I really wanted her to see me singing that song." Lucy sighed.

"Oh." Brooke gulped. "Well, she'll get to hear you sing in the chorus."

Mrs. Collins bustled toward her. "There's my star student!"

Lucy's eyes lit up, but she looked at the ground when she realized Mrs. Collins was talking to Brooke.

Izzy came over and patted her pocket. "Problem solved."

Brooke was relieved the Calla problem was under control. For now.

"We need to talk about summer music studies," Mrs. Collins said. "I can invite one student to enter the statewide competition in August. I'll tutor you myself. I just know you could win."

"Wow." Brooke wasn't sure she wanted to spend all summer singing. Ever since Calla had told her that magical creatures lived in the forest behind her house, Brooke had been looking forward to a whole summer spent exploring.

"Can you stay after school tomorrow to begin your extra lessons?" Mrs. Collins asked.

"I guess," Brooke said.

"Excellent. You're the kind of student

teachers dream about." Mrs. Collins walked back into her room, singing to herself.

Lucy ran down the hall. Brooke thought she might be crying.

After school, Brooke and Izzy dashed into the house and told her mother the good news.

"How wonderful!" Her mother hugged her. "You must've worked very hard on that song if you earned the solo."

Brooke forced a smile. "Thanks. Come on, Izzy. Let's go outside." Brooke raced to the meadow and climbed the ladder to her tree house.

"What's wrong?" Izzy came up behind her, breathless.

Brooke slumped onto the bed they used for sleepovers. "Everyone is so proud and impressed. For what? All I did was make a wish."

Izzy sat next to her and patted her back.

"But aren't you excited for everyone to see you? You'll be so popular. And maybe you'll win that competition. Heck, maybe you'll be on Broadway someday."

"That's not what I want, though. I just thought it would be fun to be the center of attention for once." Brooke stared out the window. "Now I'm just feeling like a cheater."

Calla flew over, bobbing in front of her in the air. "I'll save my comments for the book I'm writing: *When Wishes Go Wrong*. I'm sure it'll be a big seller." Calla flew over to a small desk they'd brought in from Brooke's dollhouse and started writing.

Brooke groaned. "This is just horrible. Mrs. Collins won't want me to quit. Neither will my mom. But I can't take this from Lucy, I just can't."

Izzy gave her a sympathetic look and said, "Then I guess you have to say no."

Brooke groaned. "What excuse could I possibly have for turning down the solo?"

Chapter 4

The next day during music class, Brooke came up with an amazing solution. She could sing the song horribly on purpose and Mrs. Collins would give the solo to Lucy. Today, Calla was hiding in Izzy's pocket so Izzy could take her home after school.

Brooke took a deep breath, determined to sound scratchy and out of tune, but when she sang, the song sounded just as lovely as it had yesterday. The wish had made it impossible to sing the song poorly.

When class ended, Mrs. Collins reminded her to stop by after school to start training for the summer competition. "It's going to be wonderful!"

"Great, can't wait." Brooke tried to sound excited.

At the end of the day, Brooke walked into the empty music room. Mrs. Collins patted the space next to her on the piano bench.

"I already know how well you sing 'Send Me a Rainbow.' Let's hear you sing 'Walk Through the Woods.'" Mrs. Collins opened the music book to the song and started playing. Brooke followed along with the words and sang.

After a few lines into the song, Mrs. Collins stopped playing. "You sound different."

"Do I?"

"It's not quite the same as 'Send Me a Rainbow.'" Mrs. Collins was frowning so deeply that her eyebrows were almost touching in the middle. "How odd."

Brooke sang a few more lines without the piano. She did sound different. Not bad, just not as good.

"Now sing a few lines of 'Send me a Rainbow,'" Mrs. Collins said.

So Brooke did, and once again the words flowed out beautifully.

Mrs. Collins sat quietly for a few minutes. "Let's try another song in the same key

as the rainbow song." She flipped a few pages in the music book, and started a new song.

Brooke sang along.

Mrs. Collins stopped playing. "It's still not the same." She closed the book.

"For some reason that song is just perfect for you."

Brooke suddenly realized why that song was perfect and not the others. Because she'd messed up *another* wish!

"We'll have to start with the basics. Scales, vocal exercises, breathing," Mrs. Collins said. "You've got a magical voice. We just need to figure out how to tap into it for every song."

I've got a magical voice, all right—because it was created by magic.

When the lesson was finally over, Brooke hurried home and climbed up into the tree house.

"How'd it go?" Izzy asked.

"Horrible. I'm not a great singer," Brooke said.

"What are you talking about?"

Calla grabbed her tiny quill and notebook. "Yes, tell us more."

"I wished to sing the solo perfectly. Turns out, that's *all* I can sing perfectly. Any other

song just sounds normal. I should have wished to be an amazing singer."

"Oh no!" Izzy said. "And it seemed like a perfect wish! What are you going to do?"

Brooke shrugged. "I guess I'll just sing the solo and hope wish number five works out better."

Chapter 5

The next night, Brooke stood backstage in her fanciest dress, watching the crowd fill up the auditorium and regretting her decision to leave Calla at home. It seemed too risky to let the fairy come. But Izzy was late, and Brooke could really use a friend right now!

She spotted an older Chinese woman in the front row holding a bouquet of flowers.

Brooke's mom sat a few seats down from her.

"You look very nice," Lucy told her. She was wearing a fancy dress, too.

"So do you," Brooke said. Lucy looked so sad, Brooke's heart hurt. She wanted to fake a sore throat or a stomachache and tell Lucy to take the solo. But then Brooke's mom would be so disappointed. Too bad there wasn't a wish to fix this.

Then a new idea popped into her mind. *I don't need a wish to make things right!*

She grabbed Lucy's hand. "Can you help me? I don't want to sing the solo alone. I . . . I just can't. Will you please sing it with me?"

Lucy's eyes opened wide as she smiled.

"Really?" Then her smile fell. "But you won the solo fair and square."

Brooke squeezed her hand. "It'll be better together. Please?"

Lucy giggled. "Okay!"

"And I really don't want to do the music competition. Maybe you'd like to study with Mrs. Collins instead?" Brooke asked. "We can talk to her later."

"Yes!" she cried. "I've been wishing for private singing lessons. I can't believe it. Sometimes wishes do come true!"

Brooke beamed, thrilled to play a part in granting a wish, instead of making one for herself.

The concert was just about to begin and Izzy finally appeared. Brooke felt a lot better knowing she was there, even if she was still so nervous that her stomach felt very strange.

Brooke and Lucy walked hand in hand onto the stage. Brooke felt an actual tickle on her tummy. It was more like a rumble, or a kick from a tiny creature. She pressed her hand against the bow on her dress—was that a lump? And a squeak?

Oh no! Calla had hidden in Brooke's dress! She was tucked inside the bow! But there was no time to think about it now. The crowd hushed and the lights dimmed. Mrs. Collins began to play the piano.

Lucky for Brooke that the wish made her voice come out perfectly, because she was too distracted by Calla to concentrate. What if someone in the crowd spotted a pair of wings peeking out of the bow?

Brooke and Lucy began to sing, their words joining together in the most beautiful tune. For the first time, Brooke really enjoyed singing the song.

When they finished, the audience gave them a standing ovation. Lucy threw her arms around Brooke. "Thank you so much for sharing the spotlight."

"Thank you for making it so much more fun," Brooke said.

As Brooke returned to her spot in the chorus, she quickly moved Calla to her shoulder to hide under her hair. "Stay!" she whispered.

Brooke had a hard time standing still for the rest of the concert. Calla walked back and forth across her shoulders, braided tiny sections of Brooke's hair, and sang along to some of the music. What a relief when the concert finally ended and the group filed off the stage.

Brooke's mom came over and hugged her. "You did a lovely job." Calla hung on to one of Brooke's new braids.

"Thanks, Mom." Brooke sighed with relief as her mother went to get the car without noticing the fairy.

Brooke and Izzy walked out into the cool night, Calla still riding on her shoulder.

"That was a great solution, singing with Lucy," Izzy said.

"Thanks. But now I'm really nervous to make another wish, since I screwed up that one, too," Brooke said.

"Time's running out," Calla said. "Just six more days and you've got three wishes left. What's next?"

Brooke blew out a breath, thinking. "I realize now that I didn't want the solo because I wanted to sing well. I just wanted to be popular. Can I wish for that? Can I wish for Izzy and me to be popular?"

Calla shook her head. "You can't make a wish for someone else, but you can wish it for yourself."

Brooke looked at Izzy. "If I'm popular, then you will be, too, since we're best friends."

Izzy shrugged. "That makes sense."

Brooke clapped, excited to have come up with such a good wish. "Okay, Calla, I wish I was popular!"

Calla swished her wand, and the air shimmered with glitter. "Your wish has been granted."

Brooke looked down. She was wearing the same clothes. She didn't look different or feel different. Shouldn't being popular feel awesome?

"How will you know if it worked?" Izzy asked.

"I don't know. I'm curious how long it will take," Brooke said.

As they walked to the parking lot, a group

of girls rushed toward Brooke. Calla ducked back under Brooke's hair.

"I love your new dress!" said Paige, the most popular girl in class. She'd never even talked to Brooke before.

"Thanks," Brooke said, feeling shocked.

"Want to be my partner in science?"

asked Laney, who always hung around with Paige.

"Sit with us at lunch tomorrow," said Emily, another girl from the popular table.

"Um . . ." Brooke turned to look at Izzy, but she couldn't see her. Brooke was surrounded by a circle of kids she usually didn't talk to.

As Brooke walked toward her mom's car, the girls followed. They chattered about birthday parties and end of the year celebrations.

"Sound good?" Paige asked.

"Sure." Brooke had no idea what she was agreeing with.

Brooke finally spotted Izzy and rushed over to her.

"Wow, I guess the wish worked," Izzy said.

Brooke felt giddy. "I know! This is crazy. Paige was talking to me! The wish worked! It really worked."

"It's amazing," Izzy said. "You're popular!"

"And you will be, too!" Brooke pumped her arm in the air.

Calla poked her head out from behind Brooke's hair. "This is going to be a very interesting wish to watch."

Chapter 6

The next morning, everyone in the hall said hi to Brooke and smiled at her. Emily and Paige both wanted to be her partner in gym. Several girls squealed about how much they liked Brooke's outfit.

"Thanks!" Brooke said. "But I've got to get to class!" She had to push through the crowd as the bell rang.

In science, people kept passing her notes.

"Which girl do you think is prettiest in our class?" one note said.

"This is so boring, isn't it?" another one read.

"Brooke!" the teacher snapped. "It's very important to pay attention to this lesson."

"I am. I'm sorry." Brooke's eyes stung. Teachers never yelled at her.

When Brooke sat down for lunch, several girls plopped their trays at her table. "Did you see the skirt Chelsea is wearing? It's so cute," Paige said.

"No, I didn't see it," Brooke said.

"What are you doing this weekend?" asked Emily.

Before she could answer, another girl

asked what she was having for lunch, and then Paige asked where she got her hair cut. Everyone wanted to talk to her but she couldn't get a word in edgewise!

Soon the table was full, and everyone in the cafeteria seemed to be staring at them. Brooke saw Izzy standing nearby with her tray and nowhere to sit.

"Pull up a chair." Brooke scooted over to clear a space. Izzy dragged one over, but someone else sat in it!

"I'm just going to sit over there." Izzy pointed to an empty table.

"Wait!" Brooke picked up her tray and moved next to Izzy. Then all the girls followed her to *that* table.

When the bell finally rang for the next period, Brooke realized she hadn't even had a chance to eat.

In her last class of the day, Brooke counted the minutes until the bell would ring and she could run to the bus, go home, and take a nap. She was so tired, she didn't even see that Calla had snuck out of her pocket.

Just as she noticed the fairy standing on her leg, Emily walked over and shrieked. "What is that?"

Calla froze.

"Um, well . . ." Brooke didn't know what to say.

"That is the cutest fairy doll I've ever seen." Emily reached for Calla.

Brooke quickly grabbed the still-frozen Calla. "Thanks. It was a present."

"I would love one of those. Which reminds me, I'm having a birthday party tomorrow and I want you to come!"

"I'd love to. Izzy can come, too, right?" Brooke asked.

Emily cocked her head. "Who's that?"

"My best friend. She's in our class."

Emily shrugged. "Sure, bring her along." She looked at Calla again and giggled. "That doll is just so cute!"

"Yep, she really is!" Brooke stuck Calla back in her pocket and forced a smile. This day couldn't be over fast enough!

Brooke tried on several different outfits Saturday morning, not sure what to wear to the birthday party. "I don't have many dressy clothes. Do you think it's going to be that kind of party?" she asked Izzy, who sat on her bed with Calla.

"I hope not. I'm just wearing this." Izzy gestured to her jeans and T-shirt.

Brooke shrugged. "I guess I'll pick something like that, too."

"Make sure you wear your vest so I can sit in the pocket. I'll have the perfect view from there," Calla said.

"You're coming?" Brooke asked.

"Of course! A real live human party! I need to see if the sweets are as divine as the ones back home. And I need to taste the punch—do you think there will be wildberry punch?"

"I have no idea," Izzy said. "I've never been to a party like this, either."

Calla crawled into the pocket.

"Promise you'll stay in there!" Brooke warned.

"Boring," Calla said.

"Maybe, but it's safe. You're lucky Emily believed you were just a doll when she saw you in school." Brooke turned to Izzy. "So, what did you get Emily for a present?" she asked.

"A drawing pad and colored pencils," Izzy said.

"That's nice! Mom had to take me to three stores before I found a fairy doll that looked kind of like Calla." Brooke pulled the doll out of the gift bag on her bed.

"Cute!" Izzy said. "She'll love it."

Calla zoomed out of the shirt, balled up

her fists, and planted them on her hips. "You think that raggedy thing looks like me?"

Brooke laughed. "She's not raggedy. She's just not as glorious as you. How could she be? She's not real."

Calla tipped her nose in the air. "I can't wait to see the disappointed look on that human's face when she realizes she's not getting *me*."

Chapter 7

Brooke and Izzy followed the sound of music and laughter to the backyard of an enormous brick house. A huge group of girls surrounded Emily, laughing and chatting.

"Brooke, you came!" Emily shouted, running toward her. The rest of the girls followed. They all wore fancy clothes.

Emily's eyes swept over Brooke's outfit. "Sorry, I should have told you it was a dressy party. But I thought you would know."

Brooke was happy she didn't know. She was very comfortable in what she was wearing.

"Happy birthday!" She handed Emily the gift bag.

"Happy birthday." Izzy held out her present.

"Who are you?" Emily asked.

"She's my best friend, Izzy," Brooke said.

Emily shrugged. "Well, thanks for the presents." She grabbed Brooke by the hand. "Come and see the ice sculpture my mother ordered. It's amazing!"

Brooke was pulled away from Izzy toward a table filled with fresh fruit and dips and desserts and a giant swan made out of ice.

"That's incredible!" Brooke said.

"I know. I can't wait to see what you got me," Emily said.

"You can open it now," Brooke said.

Emily pulled out the tissue paper and found the doll. Her smile fell. "It's a fairy doll. But not like the one you have."

"My grandma said it's a very rare doll. She bought it far away . . . in England . . . at a small shop." Brooke felt horrible for lying, but what else was she supposed to do? Tell Emily that she'd saved a fairy?

Emily frowned. "Okay, I understand. Come on, let's go inside so I can put her on my doll shelf."

"Let me find Izzy first," Brooke said.

"I'm sure she's fine. Don't you want to see my bedroom? I got a pet chinchilla for my birthday. He's so cute." Emily set the presents down on a table, grabbed Brooke by the hand, and dashed toward the house. "My mom said I'm not supposed to bring guests inside, but I just have to show *you*."

Brooke didn't want to leave Izzy all alone, but she would find her after she met Emily's pet.

Brooke pressed her lips together so she wouldn't gasp when they stepped inside the house. It was beautiful, with high ceilings and crystal chandeliers. She followed Emily up a curved staircase and into her bedroom, which was bigger than Brooke's family room. What would Emily think if she saw Brooke's tiny bedroom?

"Wow," Brooke whispered.

Emily set the fairy doll on a shelf with dozens of other dolls, then sat down at her desk in front of a big cage. "This is Mr. Snizzles."

Calla giggled softly inside Brooke's pocket.

"Are you laughing?" Emily asked.

"No! That's a very cool name. Can I pet him?" Brooke asked.

"No. If I open the cage, he'll run away. My mom said if he gets loose, I have to get rid of him."

Brooke leaned over to look at Mr. Snizzles. He was very cute with big ears and velvety fur.

"Do you have any pets?" Emily asked.

"A cat." A week ago, she'd had a hundred cats thanks to her first wish. She was happy to just have Patches again, though.

Emily stood and headed for the door. "We

should get back outside. Everyone is probably wondering where I am."

"Okay." Brooke followed her out the door, then heard a soft thud. She turned around and saw the chinchilla on the ground. Calla was hovering next to the open cage.

"Um, can I use your bathroom?" Brooke asked Emily as she walked down the stairs.

"Sure, it's through the door next to my bed. Then come right outside, okay?" Emily sounded a little annoyed.

"I will!" Brooke softly closed the bedroom door before hollering at Calla. "Why did you let him out?"

"I'm sure he hates living in that cage," Calla said. "I was doing him a kindness."

"Calla! We have to get him back in there

right now!" Brooke wished Izzy were there to help.

Brooke scanned the room for the cute creature. He'd disappeared. Luckily, all the doors were closed, so he had to be in the room *somewhere*. "Help me find him!"

She heard rustling sounds under the bed and dropped to her hands and knees to take a look. Big eyes stared back at her. "He's under here!"

As she reached for the pet, she noticed an open notebook peeking out from under the bed. "My Best Friends" was scrawled on top of the first page. It was dated a week earlier.

Brooke couldn't help but take a look. Emily had written down five girls from class and what she liked best about them. Brooke's name wasn't on the list. *I'd probably be on it now, right?*

But why would she be on the list? They had nothing in common. Emily was very bossy and liked dressing up. She didn't seem like the kind of girl who liked meadows and tree houses.

Calla flew up next to Brooke and then crept under the bed. "I'll lead him back to the

cage, but it seems rather cruel. You wouldn't keep *me* locked up all day, would you?"

"Of course not. I'm sure she's very kind to him. He probably enjoys being petted and cared for."

Calla lured the chinchilla out from under the bed while Brooke got the cage from Emily's desk. Mr. Snizzles followed the fairy to the cage door, and Brooke locked him back in.

"We better get back to the party." Brooke hoped Izzy had found someone to talk to.

"I want to get a closer look at the dessert table," Calla said.

"Okay. Just don't let anyone see you attacking the cupcakes!"

Chapter 8

As soon as Brooke and Calla returned to the party, several girls came up to Brooke and asked to see her fairy doll.

"I don't have it," she told them. "And I need to find Izzy." She searched everywhere in the backyard, but her best friend was harder to locate than a runaway chinchilla.

She ran up to Emily. "Have you seen Izzy?"

"The girl you came with? She left after I opened her present." Emily shrugged. "She got all upset when I told her that I don't like to draw."

Brooke bit her lip, certain that Izzy was at home, feeling bad. "I should go."

Emily put her hands on her hips. "You're going to leave my party right in the middle of everything? It's time for cake." Tears filled her eyes. "I knew something was going to go wrong today."

Brooke felt horrible making Emily upset at her party. "Okay, I'll stay a while longer."

Brooke stayed and had a slice of delicious cake, sneaking as much of it as she could to Calla. She tried to seem like she was having a good time, but she couldn't stop thinking about Izzy. She ran straight to Izzy's house after the party, but no one was there. Slowly, she walked back home.

"Does being popular mean you can only be friends with certain people?" Calla asked. "Because it doesn't seem like it's worth it, if that's the case."

Brooke said nothing and climbed the ladder to her tree house, which was lonely and boring without Izzy.

"Maybe you could invite your new friends here," Calla said.

"I'm sure they wouldn't like it. Besides, this is a special place for just me and Izzy. I don't want to share it with anyone else." She wasn't even quite sure what she *would* like to do with her new friends.

She couldn't bear to think that maybe she'd wasted yet another wish.

Sunday morning, Brooke was finishing breakfast when the phone rang.

"Hello?" she answered.

"What are you doing?" It sounded like Laney.

"Eating breakfast," Brooke said.

"Wasn't Emily's party great?" Laney rambled on for at least ten minutes, talking about the cake and the presents and the decorations.

When she finally stopped talking, Brooke said, "Okay, sounds great. See you in school tomorrow." She hung up the phone. She still had homework to do today, and she wanted to head outside.

She finished breakfast, then spent the next hour on her homework. Izzy was supposed to come over so she dashed outside. But she didn't see Izzy. Instead, Emily and Paige were walking down the road toward her house! She didn't want to hang out with

them. She and Izzy were going to look for the wisps that lived in the forest behind Brooke's house. The little creatures glowed blue when they zipped around at night, and Brooke and Izzy were curious what they looked like during the day.

Brooke dashed to the road. "Hey, what are you guys doing?"

"We came over to hang out with you," Emily said.

Brooke panicked. What were they going to do together? "Izzy and I were going to explore the woods. Want to join us?"

Paige wrinkled her nose. "You mean, out-side?"

"Yeah. That's where the woods are." Brooke laughed, but Paige and Emily didn't.

Paige shook her head. "Yuck, no."

"Yuck," Emily echoed.

Paige pulled something out of the bag slung over her shoulder. "I brought some magazines to look at. We can pick out cool clothes we want to get."

"I don't need any new clothes," Brooke said.

Emily laughed. "You're so funny, Brooke."

Just then, Izzy walked into the yard. "What's going on? Are you guys coming with us to the woods?"

Paige stepped toward her. "Oh, no, sorry. Brooke's not going to the woods today. She's hanging out with us."

Izzy's mouth dropped open, then she turned and ran back toward her house.

"Wait!" Brooke tried running after her, but Paige grabbed her arm.

"Let her go. We'll have so much more fun without her," Paige said.

"But she's been my best friend since kindergarten." Brooke fought back tears. "We've never even had a fight."

Emily shrugged. "Maybe it's time for new best friends." Emily pulled something out of her pocket. "Look, you made my list!" She unfolded the sheet from the notebook Brooke had found under her bed. Laney had been crossed out and Brooke's name was there instead.

Poor Laney! Instead of feeling flattered, Brooke thought she might cry. "I'm sorry, you guys. I have plans today. See you in school tomorrow." Brooke ran inside and slammed the door behind her.

She tried calling Izzy, but she didn't answer. Brooke was so upset, she went to her room and flopped on her bed. She stared at the ceiling, blinking back tears. She'd wished to be popular, and instead here she was—all alone.

Calla crept out of the dollhouse. "Where are all your friends?"

"I don't think those girls really are my friends. They don't like the things I like. They're mean to Izzy. Being popular isn't that great after all."

"Are you going to use a wish to undo it?"

Brooke thought for a moment. She'd messed up every wish so far, except sending those cats back to their rightful owners. What in the world would happen if she wished she wasn't popular anymore? Maybe no one would like her. "I don't think so. I'll just have to figure a way out of this without magic."

Chapter 9

The next morning when Brooke got on the bus, Izzy didn't turn to say hello. She just stared out the window as Brooke sat next to her.

"I called you yesterday, but no one answered," Brooke said.

"I didn't feel like talking," Izzy said softly. "Besides, weren't you busy with your new friends?"

"No, I didn't want to hang out with them. And they're not really my friends. Not like you are."

Finally, Izzy turned to her and smiled.

Calla crawled out of Brooke's pocket and sat on her leg. "I hope to have friends like you someday."

"You will, Calla," Brooke said. "I truly hope you find someone as great as Izzy."

Izzy beamed at her.

When they got to school, kids crowded around Brooke again, pushing Izzy aside.

Brooke had to elbow her way through the crowd to find Izzy. She grabbed her by the hand. "This is a nightmare!" Brooke said.

"I don't get it. Isn't being popular supposed to be the best thing ever?" Izzy asked.

"That's what I always thought," Brooke said. "But now I realize having you as a best friend is better than having twenty friends who don't really even know me or care about me."

"I don't like sharing you with the whole school, to tell you the truth."

Brooke flung her arms around Izzy. "I'm so lucky to have you. We'll be best friends forever and ever."

"Deal," Izzy said. "Are you going to spend a wish to fix it?"

"I've been thinking about that." Brooke tapped her chin. "I'm afraid I'll make things even worse. What if my wish made everyone hate me for the rest of my life? The way my wishes have been going, it could happen."

"True. I was a little jealous at first that you had all those wishes to make. Not any-more!" Izzy said.

"Instead of a wish, maybe I could just do something to become unpopular for a little while."

"Like what?" Izzy asked.

Brooke snapped her fingers. "I know how to fix this *and* use a wish for something awe-some instead."

"How?" Izzy asked.

"You'll see."

After the morning announcements, Mrs. Warner said, "Open your world studies books to chapter eight."

Brooke raised her hand.

"Yes?" Mrs. Warner said.

Brooke cleared her throat. "Mrs. Warner, we haven't been getting enough homework. I've been hanging out with just about everyone in class, and I think I speak for all of us when I ask you to give us more homework. Lots more."

Groans and surprised shouts filled the room.

Paige's jaw dropped. "What's wrong with you?"

Laney glared at her.

Mrs. Warner paused. "Settle down, everyone. That's an excellent idea, Brooke, especially with our final exams coming up. I'm encouraged by your interest to

learn more, class. I'll work on some new assignments for you to take home tomorrow."

Izzy stared at Brooke and raised one eyebrow. "You're definitely going to be unpopular now, but that's a pretty big price to pay," she said over the grumbling.

"Just wait," Brooke whispered. "I can fix it." She raised her hand again. "May I please use the restroom?"

"Yes, grab the pass on your way out," Mrs. Warner said.

"Can I go, too?" Izzy asked.

"Sure," Mrs. Warner said.

Brooke heard angry whispers as she and Izzy hurried out of the room.

Once the door closed behind them in the bathroom, Calla flew out of her pocket and sat on Brooke's shoulder. "You're even more unpopular than I am back in Fairvana."

"That's fine with me," Brooke said.

"Can't wait to hear what your plan is," Izzy said. "I don't want extra homework."

"You won't get any." Brooke couldn't hold back her grin. "Because I'm going to wish that Mrs. Warner stops giving our class homework."

Izzy pumped her fist in the air. "That's genius!"

"I know! Finally, a wish that's going to work out."

"So you're ready for another wish?" Calla asked.

"I sure am!" Brooke thought for a moment to get the wording right. "Calla, I wish Mrs. Warner would stop giving our class homework."

"Seems like a silly wish. Don't you enjoy reading your textbooks?" Calla asked. "They're filled with such wonderful information."

"Yes, I like learning. Just not at home. We work all day long at school," Brooke explained. "That's more than enough."

"Very well. No more homework." Calla flicked her wand, a flash of glitter filled the bathroom, and Calla said, "Your wish has been granted."

For the rest of the day, kids whispered and passed notes back and forth, and flashed dirty looks at Brooke. But it was wonderful to be left alone. No one stopped her in the halls. No one distracted her during class. She could focus all her attention on her very best friend, Izzy.

Besides, they couldn't stay mad at her forever, could they? Hopefully, over summer break, the class would forget about everything and Brooke's life would go back to normal. Sweet, wonderful normal.

A few minutes before the last bell of the day, Mrs. Warner picked up her planner. She opened it up and then closed it. "I won't be assigning any homework for tonight."

Laney raised her hand. "But Brooke asked for—"

"Shh!" Emily interrupted.

Laney put her hand down and slouched in her seat.

"Have a good evening, and see you all tomorrow," Mrs. Warner said. "Be sure you're here for the language arts exam."

Kids were smiling now, laughing and hurrying out of class. "No homework? This is great!" said several kids, high-fiving each other.

Paige glared at Brooke. "I can't believe you asked for *more* homework. And I thought you were cool." She rolled her eyes.

Emily walked by and flashed Brooke a

dirty look. "You are so lucky she didn't give us an assignment tonight."

Brooke wasn't upset at all. She ignored them and walked out of class with Izzy. "All right! Let's go home and explore."

Izzy bit her lip. "Sounds fun. But I hope I do okay on that test. We don't have any review sheets to go over tonight. If I don't keep at least an eighty average, I'll start losing privileges."

"We'll do fine," Brooke said. "We reviewed for it in class today. We don't need to study it again. Let's hunt for wood sprites. We're going to have the best time!"

Chapter 10

When they got home, Calla zoomed out of Brooke's pocket. "Wood sprites are very hard to find."

Brooke shrugged. "Searching for them will be a blast, even if we don't find them."

Calla led them to the woods behind Brooke's house. They splashed through the creek and crept into the cool, dark forest. "This is so much more fun than review sheets!" Brooke said.

Izzy hugged Brooke. "That was an amazing wish. It's helping everyone and they don't even know they should be thanking you!"

Brooke shrugged. "It was mostly so we could spend more time together."

"You really are the very best friend in the world," Izzy said.

"So are you."

"Where should we look for the sprites?" Izzy asked Calla.

"They hide right up against the trees. Sometimes on the bottom, sometimes they climb up into the branches," Calla explained.

For the next couple of hours they crept through the woods, investigating every rustle and creak they heard.

Izzy stood under a tree and gazed up at it. "I think I saw something moving. Let's climb up there." She shimmied up the trunk and Brooke followed. They searched the branches, but didn't find anything. So they sat on the branch planning out their summer.

"We have to find nymphs and a unicorn," Brooke said.

"Calla can help us!" Izzy said.

"Then I better get to work on a new book, *Helping Humans Find Magical Woodland Creatures*, because I won't be here to guide you," Calla said as she lounged on the tree branch. "My two weeks are almost up. Tomorrow, in fact."

Brooke frowned. "I forgot that you'll

be leaving soon. I'm going to miss you so much."

"And I will miss you," said Calla. "My time here has been very informative. And I never thought . . ."

"What?"

"I never thought that I'd become friends with humans," Calla said.

Brooke held out a finger and Calla hopped on. "And I never dreamed I'd become good friends with a fairy."

Izzy laughed. "Me either. We better get home before it gets dark."

"You're right." Brooke climbed down the tree. "We didn't find a wood sprite, but I still had tons of fun." It had been a delightful afternoon they wouldn't have gotten to spend together if she hadn't made that wish. *Finally, one that worked out perfectly!*

When Brooke went inside, her mom crossed her arms and looked angry. "It's about time you came in. You need to get your homework done."

"We don't have any," Brooke said.

Her mom's eyebrows rose. "That's strange. You always have a bit of work to do."

Brooke shrugged. "Not today. I'm going to watch TV!" Brooke spent the rest of the night doing whatever she wanted—all because of her wonderful wish!

The next morning, Mrs. Warner started class with the language arts test. Brooke answered the first two questions easily, but got stuck on question three. And four and five. She tapped her eraser on the desk. *I know we talked about this in class, but I just can't remember it.*

She left several questions blank, and went over them again and again until Mrs. Warner said, "Time's up!"

Mrs. Warner collected the test papers. "I'll grade these tonight. And don't forget the math test tomorrow."

"Ugh, I'm not looking forward to that," Izzy said.

"I don't like division, either," Brooke said. "At least we won't have to do any homework tonight."

"Best wish ever!" Izzy whispered, holding up her hand for a high five.

Brooke worried for a moment, remembering how hard the language arts test had been. But she was good at math. She'd probably be fine without any review sheets. "Can't wait to get home and have more fun!"

Chapter 11

"We have the whole afternoon to explore again. What should we do today?" Brooke asked Izzy as they walked home.

Izzy thought for a moment. "Yesterday, Calla took us exploring in the woods. Maybe we should take Calla exploring in town. I can think of a few places she'd like to visit."

"So can I!" Brooke said.

Calla flew out of Brooke's pocket. "Where? Will it be yummy?"

"You'll have to wait and see. Let's get our bikes!" Izzy said.

They rode their bikes into town, past the library and the park.

"Stay hidden on my shoulder," Brooke said as they parked their bikes in front of the ice-cream parlor.

Calla flew up onto her shoulder and sighed. "This place smells divine."

The bells jingled as they walked inside.

"We'd like to share a great big sundae," Brooke told the man working behind the counter.

"In a waffle bowl," Izzy added.

"With chocolate and vanilla ice cream and sprinkles!" Brooke said.

Calla squealed.

"Was that you?" the man asked. "Are you all right?"

Brooke nodded. "Yes, I'm just excited."

"What's hot fudge? Can we have that?" Calla whispered in Brooke's ear.

"We'd like hot fudge, please," Brooke added.

"And whipped cream and M&M's?" Calla requested.

"Just give us all your toppings, please," Brooke said.

The man paused. "Are you sure?"

"Very sure." Izzy giggled. "My mom said I should only have a little, but it'll be great!"

"Can we have two regular spoons and one sample-sized spoon?" Brooke asked.

The man looked confused. "Isn't the sample spoon too small?"

"No. We have a small friend who is really going to enjoy this," Izzy said with a smile.

They took the sundae to the park and sat by the pond sharing the delicious treat.

"We'll call this sundae the Calla Special!" Brooke said.

"Yum!" Calla flew loop-de-loops and spun in the air as she gobbled down the sundae.

"You've eaten so much of this, I'm surprised you can even fly!" Brooke laughed.

When they finished, they lay back on the grass and watched the clouds pass.

"What a perfect afternoon." Izzy sighed.

"I know. But we'd better go home . . . and not do homework!" Brooke giggled.

As Brooke walked into her house, with Calla tucked in her pocket, her mom stomped out of the kitchen. "Your teacher just called."

"Really? Why?" Brooke asked.

Her mom put her hands on her hips. "To let me know all of the students in class failed today's test—including you!"

Brooke's jaw dropped open. "Failed?" she whispered.

Her mother nodded. "I don't understand why you didn't study for it?"

Brooke bit her lip. "Because she didn't give us any homework."

"You have a math final tomorrow, don't you?" her mom asked.

Brooke nodded.

"Make sure you study for that," her mother said. "Another bad grade, and you're going to lose privileges."

Brooke went to her room and flopped on her bed. Calla flew out of her pocket.

Brooke sighed. "I can't study. I didn't bring home my math book and I don't have any review sheets because I wished for no homework!"

"You have one wish left—and you need to make it by tomorrow," Calla reminded her. "Do you want to wish for your review sheets?"

Brooke thought for a moment. That would be a horrible last wish. She shook her head. "No, I'll figure something out." But what?

Chapter 12

The next morning, Brooke gave Calla a handful of chocolate chips. "That should keep you busy. You'll have to stay here today. I need to concentrate at school. Can you stay out of trouble?"

"Of course." Calla shrugged. "I'll work on my book in the tree house."

Brooke sat next to Izzy on the bus. "Want to ride bikes after school?"

"I can't," Izzy said. "I'm grounded because

of my bad test grade. If I don't get my final average up, I'll be grounded all summer!"

"Oh, I'm so sorry!" Brooke said.

"I better do well on that math test," Izzy said.

When they walked into class, all the students were quiet, many of them frowning.

"What's wrong?" Brooke asked.

Emily's shoulders slumped. "I failed yesterday's test and I'm grounded."

Paige crossed her arms and pouted. "I can't watch TV for the rest of the week."

"I might have to go to summer school because of that test yesterday," said a boy sitting nearby.

Brooke gulped. She never imagined this would happen!

"I thought Mrs. Warner was going to give us more homework, not less," Paige said.

A boy in the back of the room raised his hand. "Can you please give us some study sheets for the science test tomorrow? Something we can take home tonight?"

Mrs. Warner chuckled. "I don't think you need any homework. We already went over it in class. Besides, I'm enjoying not grading so many papers."

Brooke panicked. She needed to study for the science test. And she should have studied for the math test today! But Mrs. Warner was refusing to send them home with work—thanks to her wish. *Another wish that had gone horribly wrong in the end!*

How was she going to fix this one? If she wished to start getting homework again, they might get too much of it. And asking for it didn't help. Mrs. Warner had already said no!

Then she got a great idea.

She raised her hand and asked, "Could we have some math review sheets to look over . . . during *lunch*?" That way, they could study before the test that afternoon.

Mrs. Warner thought for a moment, then shrugged. "Sure, if you want to. I've got some right here. Who would like one?"

Every hand in the room shot up.

Brooke remembered the other test coming up, too. "Do you have one for the science test tomorrow?"

"Of course. If you want extra work, you just need to ask for it," Mrs. Warner said.

Everyone asked for a science study sheet, too. All the students spent their lunch working together and filling in the sheets.

When Mrs. Warner passed out the math test after lunch, Brooke felt nervous. But

then she quickly worked through all the problems. She aced it for sure.

Mrs. Warner collected everyone's test sheets. "I certainly hope these are better than yesterday's test. I'll grade them during recess. Go out and have fun."

Izzy raised her hand. "Can we stay inside during recess and do some more sheets for our other tests?"

"Sure, if you'd like," Mrs. Warner said, sounding puzzled.

Every student in class quietly worked on their review sheets instead of running out to the playground.

When the recess period ended, Mrs. Warner passed out their tests. "Good work, class. Everyone passed!"

Brooke pumped her arm in the air when she saw her grade. "One hundred percent!"

"I got a ninety!" Izzy said.

But there was still the problem of that horrible language arts test grade.

Before the bell rang at the end of the day, Brooke got a great idea. "Is there any extra work we can do to bring up our language arts grades?" she asked the teacher. "Since we all failed that test?" She felt so bad that her classmates were in trouble—because of her.

Mrs. Warner thought for a moment. "I had the last two days of school reserved for a party and movies, but if you'd prefer to do extra credit, I can arrange that for interested students."

Brooke breathed a huge sigh of relief. It looks like she was able to fix another bad wish.

"Thank goodness it's almost the end of the school year," Brooke said to Izzy as they stopped at Brooke's house that afternoon. "I'm pretty sure things will go back to normal next year. I asked for Mrs. Warner to stop giving our class homework. So it only applies to our teacher, and our class. Next year, we'll have a different teacher and she'll have a different class, so the wish won't be in effect. Thankfully, I got the wording all wrong on that one, too."

"It seemed like such a good idea," Izzy said.

"All of them did," Brooke said, heading for the meadow. "At first."

Calla flew out of the tree house and bobbed in the air in front of them. "Welcome home! How did you do on your test?"

"Great!" Brooke and Izzy said at the same time, laughing.

"You know, it's your last day to make your final wish," Calla said.

Brooke shook her head. "No thanks. My wishes didn't work out the way I wanted them to. I don't want to risk causing any more problems. I'll skip the last wish."

Calla fluttered her wings and crossed her

arms, pouting. "But you can't! I have to grant you seven wishes in a fortnight. Those are the rules. So you need to come up with something."

Brooke shrugged. "I can't think of anything I want. I don't need anything. Getting these wishes made me realize my life is already great. I've got the very best friend in the whole wide world."

Izzy smiled at her.

"I've got a family that loves me, an awesome pet, a great big backyard to explore, and I've got a fairy for a friend. Honestly, what else could I want?"

Calla sighed. "I don't know. But think of something. How can I finish my book on wishes if you don't make all of yours? I can't

return to Fairvana with a tale of the six wishes I granted. The other fairies will think I'm not a good wish granter."

Brooke didn't like thinking about Calla leaving so soon and returning to Fairvana. "I'm going to miss you, Calla." Suddenly Brooke's eyebrows rose, and she sucked in a deep breath. "Oh my gosh. I can't believe I didn't think of this before."

"What?" asked Izzy. "You came up with something?"

"Yes. It would be incredible. I don't even know if you can grant it, Calla. But it would be the most amazing wish ever!" Brooke said.

"I'm up for the challenge," Calla said, rubbing her hands together. "What is it?"

Brooke tried not to squeal. "Calla, I wish . . ."

The magic continues...
Turn the page for a sneak peek at

#4 Fairies Forever

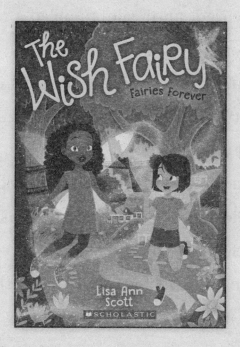

Izzy bounced on her toes, clutching her hands in front of her. "Please, please, make the wish!"

Brooke cleared her throat. "Calla, I want to visit Fairvana with you and Izzy. Right now."

"Seriously? Woo-hoo!" Izzy squealed and twirled until she tumbled onto the flowery field.

Calla's eyes were wide. "I wasn't expecting that."

"But you can do it, right?" Brooke asked.

Calla landed on the big flat rock in the field. She paced back and forth, thinking.

Patches and Izzy's cat, Pumpkin, charged through the field and jumped onto the rock next to her.

Calla squeaked in surprise, but the cats just curled up next to her. The fairy patted Pumpkin's tail affectionately. She was no longer deathly afraid of the cats like she had been at first.

"I suppose I can grant that wish," Calla said. "I imagine all the fairies will be so excited to see real humans, maybe they'll finally want to be friends with me!" She flew up into the air and spun around. "Go ahead, then, make your wish!"

Welcome to the
ENCHANTED PONY ACADEMY,
where dreams sparkle and magic shines!